PRAISE FOR NICOLA LOMBARDI

"This can't-look-away weird tale begins a little like an urban crime-noir, with its naïve grimdark character who cannot pay his debts but quickly devolves into something macabre and twisted. Written in a traditional style perfectly suited to the gothic nature of the narrative and with some truly scary elements, the story features themes of social inequality and betrayal. I love the 'surreal' metaphor of Magritte here since things are clearly not all they seem throughout this little page-turner. Not for the squeamish!"
—Lee Murray

"An expert connoisseur of literary and cinematic horror, Nicola Lombardi is one of the most highly regarded and talented writers of contemporary horror, capable of probing the darkest recesses of the human soul through a lens--at the same time both true and distorting--as only the finest writers know how to do."
—*Guida ai narratori italiani del fantastico* (Odoya Editore, 2018)

"Lombardi, a veteran of literary horror, manages to describe distressing psychological moments, delving into the most underground meanderings of the subconscious with great skill . . . Lombardi writes words and phrases in such a fascinating way that it captures you from the very first description."
—*Progetto Babele*

"One of the most important Italian authors of the macabre . . . esteemed both in Italy and abroad."
—Christian Sartirana

"Nicola knows how to spread his magic to any reader thanks to an impressive elegance, a grace worthy of high literature, chiseling supernatural horrors with perfect and clean language."
—*Paolo Di Orazio*

CLUB MAGRITTE

NICOLA LOMBARDI

Translated by
J. WEINTRAUB

CLUB MAGRITTE

Edited by Holly Lyn Walrath.

Cover design by Holly Lyn Walrath

Published by Interstellar Flight Press

Houston, Texas.

www.interstellarflightpress.com

ISBN (Print): 978-1-953736-49-9

ISBN (EBook): 978-1-953736-48-2

First Edition: 2025

CONTENTS

CLUB MAGRITTE

"Hey, buddy, got a light?"

It took only three seconds for Mauro to recognize the voice. He was walking along a sidewalk faintly lit by the dusty beam seeping from a streetlamp, and without ever looking into his face, he instinctively came to a halt next to the figure who had spoken to him. Only after he had slipped his hand into the pocket of his threadbare coat did he raise his eyes. Three seconds too late. But in either case, he would not have had time to get away.

Five thick fingers closed like a vise around his collar, forcing him to rise up on his toes and clench his teeth. Only by a miracle was the tip of his tongue not caught between his incisors. Immediately after, the other five fingers, closing into a fist, cut through the night air to slam into the pit of his stomach. A stifled choking sound burst from his throat as he tried in vain to bend forward and fall. His assailant then pushed him into the dark belly of the alley where he had been lying in wait for Mauro to leave the bar, and with shocking force, he shoved him against the splintered bricks of a wall.

Another person was also there with them. Mauro caught

sight of his presence as he was whirled about from the sallow, yellowish glow of the street into almost total blackness, and, in his mind, the entire situation became clear to him, as if someone had just explained it to him, calmly, step by step. He should have expected it. Certainly, no one else was then wandering about around there, not in that neighborhood, not at almost one in the morning. And even if someone had noticed what was happening, that someone never ever would have interfered. Obviously not.

The hot, foul breath of the man who had taken him by surprise was exhaled into his face from only a few inches away, a distance measured by the width of the brim of the borsalino worn by the thug, a distinctive accessory belonging to his kind.

"The Duke was waiting for you tonight. At ten. At the appointed spot."

Mauro tried to reply, but the pain radiating within his belly and chest made it impossible for him to turn the few words he had in his mouth into sounds. Besides, the hand with which Gandhi continued to tighten his collar acted as an additional, and by no means slight, hindrance. He then thought of relying on gestures, moving his hands in a sequence of quick jerks, and he got the desired result as the grip on his collar loosened, and it was possible for him to place his heels again on the ground.

He was not aware of Gandhi's real name, but it was enough to know that everyone called him that. He was one of the Duke's henchmen, and like all of the witty nicknames, this one had very likely been pinned on him as a clear and absolute contrast, both in the matter of body weight and tendency toward violence. He wasn't what would be termed a giant (he was a little over six feet, although he stood several inches over Mauro), but he had a physique that would have convinced anyone to classify him as a bouncer or a hired brawler. And that, in fact, is what he was. And now he was there for Mauro, with a message to deliver. He had waited for him with all the patience that only the bearers of bad news know how to display and, finally, he had gotten him.

"I know, I know," Mauro said, coughing and raising his eyes in a failed attempt to read the expression on the other's face. Gandhi had a very limited range of expressions. Or, to be just, he had a pair of them: the impassive one, of a wooden statue that never suggested the glimmer of a thought or emotion; and the one of vague amusement that led him to draw the corners of his mouth into a satisfied grin whenever he had the chance to inflict pain. But whatever expression was shaping his features at that moment, it was unreadable in the shadows that cut off more than half of his face.

"You know? And what is it that you know? That you've gotten yourself into a heap of trouble? Not much doubt about that, my friend."

Gandhi seemed intent on crushing him against the wall. Mauro turned his eyes toward the entrance of the alleyway, as if he could count on someone intervening. At that moment, he saw again the other man's back, the one who now seemed to be keeping watch. Thin, with a hat, a little too large for him and tilted to one side, he was keeping his hands deep inside the pockets of his long overcoat. As far as Mauro knew, it could have been anyone. Still, he should not have expected any help from there.

"When someone owes the Duke money," continued Gandhi in the meantime, "and then doesn't show up at the appointed hour to pay him back, he's taking a step that would be an understatement to define as a simple mistake. It is an action that makes no sense whatsoever. It's like holding your breath and waiting to see what'll happen next. Do you understand what I'm saying?"

Mauro nodded, as the absurd notion passed through his head that this massive goon spoke an articulate and imaginative language, opposite to what he would have been led to believe judging just from his appearance. The Duke had likely sent him for that, too. He could count on the service of several thugs, but probably Gandhi was the one who would have known best how to convey the spirit of his message.

"Yes, yes . . . I understand," he managed to sputter out. "And I assure you . . . I assure you I have every intention of paying . . . It's just that . . ."

"Ah, here we are, we've come to the 'It's just that . . .' So, let me guess. You don't have the seven grand you owe him."

Mauro wrinkled his brow. "It's five . . . it's five thousand."

A bitter laugh burst from Gandhi's mouth. "No, no, my friend. The Duke sent me to tell you it's seven thousand now. Did you really think that this transgression of yours didn't actually have a price? Others have had a little more seasoning, too, you know, and even more of it. I'd say you're getting off pretty lightly. For right now, anyway."

Mauro saw a trail of reddish spots, like the wake of a tiny comet, pass across his retina as all the thoughts he was trying to put in order inside his head merged instantly into a tangled mess. Should he say something? Or should he wait to hear if there was anything else? Despite the chilly temperature, it seemed to him his body was burning beneath the onslaught of an unnatural fever.

Gandhi, however, did not give him time to recover from the shock, and he passed without delay to the final part of his message. "Listen to me carefully. That seven thousand has to be delivered within forty-eight hours at the place and time you already know. No deviations permitted. You do know what 'deviation' means, don't you?"

Mauro nodded emphatically, and at that point, Gandhi broke off all physical contact with him. Taking a step backward, he rubbed the palms of his hands together and brushed off his coat with their backs as if, up until that moment, he had been dealing with a pile of garbage. But, clearly, he was not yet finished, since he kept staring into the eyes of his victim.

"One final thing. Very important."

Mauro, who was massaging his Adam's apple, froze once again.

"As you can imagine, for the Duke, the seven thousand you owe him is no more than chicken feed, but it's annoying, and gambling debts have to be honored, always. Even if we were talking only about a hundredth of that. Still, the chief knows you don't have that kind of cash, although you wanted to play with it anyway, so he assigned me to prove his generosity to you by offering you some help."

Without looking around, he pointed with his thumb to the lanky figure at the entrance of the alleyway, who was continuing to keep his back toward them. "That's Ruben. Second cousin to the Duke. He's here to give you some really valuable information. That is, if you care to have seven stacks of green in your hands within two days."

As if it were impossible for him to keep a respectful distance, and imagining, perhaps, a revolver in his grip, Gandhi lifted his hand and jabbed a high-caliber fingertip into Mauro's chest. "In the case of a second missed payment, the Duke has given me leave to do with you whatever gives me the most satisfaction, and, so, you should know that—"

A high nasal voice, one with authority, cut through the shadows. "Keep it short, Gandhi. He gets it. You can go now. Thanks."

Ruben had not turned toward them but had merely swiveled his head around in a way that would carry his few words to their target without any misunderstanding. Gandhi, looking abruptly toward the alley's opening, seemed to reflect for a moment over the charge he had been given, and then he turned his eyes back on Mauro, as he withdrew his finger from his chest. Probably a few choice parting words would have suited him, but the Duke's cousin had caught him off guard, so he simply nodded and, affecting a slow pace, began to move off.

Mauro, recognizing at once the command structure between the two, and now feeling relatively protected, could not hold back, "Be seeing you around, Gandhi!"

It was a mistake, as was the case with most of his ventures.

The thug reversed himself with the speed of an enraged bull, and for the second time, his fist met the same target but with decidedly superior force.

A wheezing gurgle sputtered from Mauro's mouth, and he folded over himself, collapsing to one side. A trashcan and some foul, sodden boxes greeted him as he staggered downward, slowing his fall a little.

"Only someone who's got my permission can talk to me like that, asshole!"

Mauro heard Gandhi's voice, through clenched teeth, gushing over him from above. Then the sounds of his steps faded away, while through half-closed eyes he barely picked up the variations in light brought about by the movement of forms and shadows. One man was going away, and another was drawing near.

An imaginary drill was boring through the space between his temples, and in his solar plexus, a second heart, made of lava, was beating. A terrible taste filled his mouth, and it was then that Mauro realized he had vomited. His nostrils were permeated with the smell of sour beer, combined with the sweetish gases of spoiled fruit and other garbage released by the invisible cloud into which he had collapsed. He tried coughing to clear his airways, but a new surge of nausea forced him to curl up into an even tighter fetal position. And with a remaining patch of still lucid thought, he managed to curse himself for his own inescapable stupidity.

He felt a hand settling on his shoulder. Someone beside him was leaning over. It must be that Ruben.

"Get with it, man, get up! No one, as far as I know, ever died from a punch to the gut. Come on. You and I have to talk."

Mauro allowed the stranger to help lift him up, and on slightly uncertain legs, he got to his feet once again. With his sleeve, he wiped off the foul-smelling liquid that was dripping down one cheek. Risking a "thank you" as he considered whether anything else was about to rise up his throat, he looked at the man who was standing by his side and still loosely holding a hand in the hollow of his armpit to support him.

"Can I call you Ruben?" Better to tread lightly, he thought, given what had just happened to him.

The other smiled beneath the broad-brimmed hat sloping sideways across his head. "Why not? It's my name."

"Have you ever heard of Club Magritte?"

Ruben accompanied him as Mauro retraced his steps, slipping into the same bar where he had just spent, as was his habit, several unproductive and stupid hours. The place was about to close, as Mauro had warned his companion, but that did not disturb him. The bartender—an almost obese, middle-aged man, with thinning, greasy-slick hair—had immediately glared at the two, as was expected, and from his mouth came several unkind words. But as soon as Ruben had spoken ("My friend's not feeling well, and we need to take it easy for a short half-hour. Do you think we can do that?") and had taken off his hat, the barkeep opened his eyes wide and was full of apologies. He must have recognized him. Sure, Ruben was one of the Duke's men. And not only that, he was one of his relatives. And so, the two unexpected guests were seated at a small table beneath a dirty overhead lamp that gave off just enough of an orange glow of light to allow them to look into each other's face. The rest of the bar was deserted, with several chairs already overturned, pointing with their long, woody fingers toward a darkness, reeking of alcohol and smoke, stagnating across the ceiling.

The question that Ruben had directed at him, point-blank, circled about a couple of times in Mauro's brain in search of some resonant memory. Not finding any, he was forced to shake his head.

"Two beers, please," said Ruben, directing his order toward the motionless and barely discernible figure of the bartender, prudently lurking behind his counter. Mauro snorted a bit of a giggle from out of his nostrils. It already seemed to be a big deal to him that the barkeep had let them come in and sit down, even though he was almost at the point of lowering the shutters. And now this Ruben took the liberty of ordering two beers! But that, actually, was not very surprising. Everyone knew the Duke, and no one would have wanted to make an enemy of him.

The beers arrived within ten seconds. Ruben thanked the man respectfully, even if such deference was entirely pointless, but then he added, "Now, please, take off into the back. We have to talk over some important things, very private. I'll call you when we're ready to leave, okay?"

The barkeep did not say a word. He only raised the thumb of his right hand, nodded, and vanished with a rustling sound behind a folding door, closing it after him.

"Okay, so . . . prosit!" Ruben grabbed the tall glass, leaving a small, moist ring on the faded tray that once must have been green, and he took a deep and satisfying draft. Mauro did not really feel the need to do the same, but the look the other was sending his way was a clear and firm signal to follow his lead. He then allowed the cold and bitter liquid to flow down and fill the void in his stomach, praying that it would stay there. In the meantime, he began to size up his new drinking companion as he wondered where all this was heading.

Ruben was about forty, forty-five years old. He was lean physically, with tight features, almost free of wrinkles. His straight hair, a very light brown, was combed back over his wide forehead, and the gaze from his watery, blue eyes conveyed a sense of intelligence and authority. His thin nose overhung a colorless and unkempt mustache, while his lips seemed subject to a barely perceptible tremor, as if a constant muscular twitch was preventing them from curling into a sneer. Mauro began to think that, altogether, the guy reminded him in some way of Fred Astaire.

"That Gandhi's an idiot," remarked Ruben abruptly. "I've known him for years. Brutal as they come, but always bolstered by an entirely personal view of the work he's called upon to carry out. The problem is he's seen Tarantino's films too many times. And when he goes off on a tangent, he can keep talking until the end of time."

Mauro managed to smile for the first time in days. "Yeah, I've noticed that."

Ruben, having become suddenly serious, looked him straight in the eye. "But you're an idiot, too, or am I wrong?"

Taken by surprise, Mauro drew his head back. Then, however, he shook it lightly to the left and to the right, as if to say, "Well, all in all, I get by . . ."

"You've taken advantage of the Duke's trust, you've incurred a very heavy debt, and you haven't honored it, even though you were given a week to scrape together the cash. I don't know if you realize it, but others in your place would already be making a close study of the flora and fauna of the bottom of some river."

Mauro kept quiet, having become aware of his own sweat and the odors from his body.

"Yours is a rather ugly predicament. Not the very worst, since I'm here with you on this, but still, yes, rather ugly. I don't know much about your affairs, but from what little I've been told, your prospects for a future life, if you don't find some reasonable way out, are not very great. Do you agree?"

Mauro nodded silently, and dropped his eyes shamefully toward the inside of his glass, losing himself in the amber liquid and the infinitesimal concentric circles on its surface provoked by the trembling in his hand.

———

Mauro Ridolfi, thirty-two years old, did not have a steady job, and no romantic attachments, at least not at the moment. Behind him were a marriage and a live-in girlfriend—experiences that never managed to celebrate a second anniversary—and both had left him with few marks, but by his very nature, he was incapable of dragging along problems or low spirits for very long. With Sylvia, his wife, he was convinced, at the beginning, that it could last forever. But he had not taken into account the thousand temptations that life would maliciously place under his nose. Not that he really had a thousand chances to prove his own infidelity: already by the second, he had found his suitcases waiting for him outside the door. With Beatrice, the relationship had been a little looser, on both sides. He did not feel the pressure imposed by marriage ties, but at the same time, he had to learn to deal with the possibility that other men could, with ease, be blowing their noses, so to speak, into his handkerchief. It was not, however, jealousy that had put an end to that affair, but rather the fact that eventually Beatrice had come to understand what stuff he was made of, or to use some of her favorite terms, that he was a "loser," a "good-for-nothing," and, not infrequently, "a moron to the nth power." So be it. Still, no kids, thank God. He never wondered if it were his fault, or his partner's, or perhaps it was only a matter of luck. Quite simply, he had not left any little Mauros hanging around, and that was good enough for him.

He had returned to live at home for a few years with his mother, a retired mathematics teacher in her early seventies. For a short time, in the past, they had benefited from the disability payments his father collected after being almost electrocuted atop a high-voltage pylon during a negligent repair operation. Then, after his father's death, Mauro and his mother had learned to live off her retirement pension, at least during the times Mauro found himself without work.

In his life, he had done a bit of everything—from gas station attendant, to waiter; from supermarket clerk to managing a newsstand—but he had hardly ever known how to keep those jobs for more than six months. To listen to him, it was always his supervisor's fault—too demanding, or too strict, or always too something. But the truth was much simpler: Work didn't much agree with him. Before long, he had been branded by many as a "misfit," and however degrading a name like that could be, there were too many factors and circumstances confirming its validity.

"Dear Mauro, you're really such a misfit." Those words, so simple, so blunt, had been uttered one day even by his mother, in cold blood, after yet another firing. She had not said it out of meanness, but from a sort of bitter resignation, and it was probably that undertone that made her remark so irritating, as pointless as it may have been.

In the past, Mauro had also had some fleeting contact with the underworld—dealing light drugs, illegal betting—but he got out of it in time. Criminality was not his kind of thing, and the thought of ending up in the cooler always held him back. Certainly, easy money was to be made there, as some particular friends often told him, but taking refuge behind the vague idea of a moral code, Mauro preferred to beach himself on green velvet shores—gambling, more or less—to supplement the check he collected from the post office every month for his mother, that is, when things were going well.

His contact with the Duke's circle had happened rather recently, and it was exactly at the seventh session that he was struck by disaster. Up to that moment, he had visited with passable diligence—and passable bad luck—the slots and video poker machines near the front of the houses, and was only sporadically committed to challenging flesh-and-blood players. Rarely did he have significant cash available, and this fact—along with his notable "misfitness"—did not make him a particularly welcome gambler. Only after his continued insistence with the friend of a friend of a friend did the Duke finally agree to have him sit at one of the tables in one of the three gambling houses he ran in the area. The Duke was . . . how could he be described? Capo? Lord? Godfather? All the local activity tied to drugs, gambling, and prostitution invariably passed under his control and the coalition of families he represented. To get into the Duke's good graces was certainly an honor as well as a guarantee of safety, and being accepted to play poker with him and his shady cronies had been a source of immense pride for Mauro. Until he ran headlong into grim reality.

Good cards were coming up in the Duke's house. Over the course of six sessions played in three days, through highs and lows, Mauro had scraped together a sum equal to his mother's monthly check, and in that cursed night from a week before, he had, with a light heart, decided to challenge fate and his fellow gamblers again after they had insisted so much on him continuing to play with them. If he had been smart, he would have found some excuse to disappear. But since he was who he was—in the jargon of the day, a "pigeon"—he had smiled and returned to sit down in front of the Duke. And so, the noose tightened around his neck.

The tactic was firmly established. During the previous sessions, he had been fed the illusion of being a formidable—and most certainly a lucky—player, an illusion that after the first two or three hands of the seventh match crumbled like dry bread. He had begun by having his stake eaten up a little at a time, until he had wiped it out, and then he went underwater, always deeper . . .

The unraveling of the final hand would then be repeated in his head a hundred times, perhaps with the hope that at least in his imagination it could end differently. But the Duke and his henchmen played along with his pitiful bluff. One raise after the next, until the Duke had pronounced the fatal words, "I'll see you." And the busted inside straight quivering between Mauro's scorched fingers was instantly turned into a debt of five thousand euros.

Or rather, seven thousand now, since he had tried to play the wise guy with the Duke. Naturally, he had every intention of paying. Could he ever have thought, as much of a misfit as he was, of ripping off the Duke? Certainly, he did not have all of that money, right then and there. He could have sold something: watches, antique prints, vintage comics. . . Except that he had already turned toward that sort of solution, and extensively. And, putting himself in the hands of a loan shark seemed to him to be pure suicide. He had heard about people getting stuck down the rathole of usury, and some of those had not come out of it alive. Besides, the circle of loansharking, whichever way it spun, inevitably wound up with the Duke and his crew, so that route had been rejected outright. He would pay in installments and, sure, that passed through his head. He would set something aside every month, preventing women and the slots from eating everything up. He would . . . he would . . . Ultimately, he simply did not show up at the appointed time. A brilliant move. From a true misfit.

He had slipped into a bar, the one he was in at the current moment, and had let time go by as he nursed a beer, watching the miserable players lost behind their cards, their greasy cardboard rectangles, being shuffled between sweaty fingers, slapped down on the plastic tablecloth, their suits, numbers, figures fading before his eyes . . . until he felt himself drifting away into drowsiness, nausea, and the impatience over what he continued to consider to be his life, the only one he had and would continue to have.

And it was then he decided to leave, and to go home . . . and to be brought rudely back to earth by Gandhi.

———

"And so, since the Duke knows how desperate you are, he asked me to offer you a reasonable solution. Club Magritte, to be exact."

Mauro resurfaced, troubled, from the bottom of the glass where he had let his mind sink for a few seconds, and with his red, swollen eyes, he stared at this strange companion of his. He would not have minded had he started to cry. Perhaps it would have relieved him somewhat from the weight of his own self.

"Let's hear it," he limited himself to saying. A mouthful of sour staleness threatened to rise up from his throat, but he held it back with a raspy cough.

"Okay, Mauro, I'll see if I can keep it short and, above all, clear." Ruben leaned forward and lowered his voice, even if nothing more than a gloomy gulf of darkness surrounded them. "This Club is based in a huge mansion in the hills, about twenty miles from here. The founder, the lord and master of all of this, is a man named Augusto Lambertini. A patron of the arts, noble family, filthy rich."

Mauro heard himself asking, "Magritte . . . like the painter?"

"Yeah, René Magritte. Lambertini is a great fan of painting and of Magritte, in particular. But what they're doing at the Club has very little to do with art. Or maybe someone could even see something artistic in it; anything is possible. They're a peculiar lot. I know that, because I'm also a part of it."

Mauro watched him in silence. His heart had quickened its pace. Where was this conversation going?

With a second swallow, Ruben emptied his glass, and he raised his left hand, which up until then—as Mauro realized just at that moment—had remained hidden beneath the table. He then placed it conspicuously in front of him. It was missing the little and the ring fingers. In their place were two bony protuberances—visible, but just barely—covered with a layer of bruised and shriveled skin.

Mauro took in the sight, and he again lifted his eyes to meet those of Ruben.

The man was carelessly drumming his three remaining fingers on the tabletop. "What they do at Club Magritte is, in essence . . ." He lowered the volume of his voice even further to complete the sentence. ". . . well, they eat people."

Mauro shifted back against the chair, letting slip the hint of a smile and a faint whistle as a sign of surprise, or shock.

"Now," continued Ruben, "don't jump to hasty conclusions. It's a complicated matter, involving millions of euros in annual revenue activity."

"Those two fingers . . ." whispered Mauro, pointing to the stumps.

"Yes, my . . . they were eaten. One by Lambertini in person, and the other by a newcomer to the Club. I needed the money. I was comfortable with seven thousand a finger, to get me out of a thorny situation. I think you can understand me."

Mauro nodded. "Seven thousand . . ."

"Yes, in cash. On the nail, if you'll allow me a little play on words."

"But, what's the point? I mean, why do they do it?"

Ruben smiled. "Why do they do it? Who? Those doing the eating? Or those who allow themselves to be eaten? And 'why' is a complicated matter, as I told you. Anthropophagy is a perversion that has very deep roots. Even the inactive kind. The so-called 'eaten' do it for the money, while the 'eaters' are willing to pay out staggering sums to satisfy their desires. What I mean is, it gets them off. Again, there are some peculiar types in the Club, like I said."

At that point he paused, making a careful study of Mauro's expression. This phase of the transaction was a decidedly delicate one.

After a brief reflection, as he absorbed Ruben's last words, Mauro ran a hand through his hair, slowly massaging his scalp. "In effect, what you're proposing to me . . ."

"I'm offering you a way to save your skin. You've got nothing left to sell, or to pawn, nor are you the type who can manage to get ahold of seven thousand euros with a robbery or something like that, and that's a fact. And, all the people who could, in theory, lend you that sum recognize who you are, and you know very well they wouldn't put up even seven of those euros for you. Your postal account, or rather your mother's, isn't of any help to you, and no, don't give me that look. I know a few things, and that's that. To cut to the quick, if the day after tomorrow you don't deliver that amount into the Duke's hands, or whoever is there for him, you're a dead man. And that's the truth. There's no more to it, and you know that better than I do."

Another pause, which was spent listening to far-off cries, automobile engines, and a dog's howling that was much too similar to the wailing of a child lost in the night. Mauro began again with the phrase that had been cut short in his mouth. "You're proposing that I let . . . that I let a finger of mine be eaten by these people, am I right?"

"Plain and simple, that's what it is."

"For seven thousand euros . . ."

Mauro caught himself looking at his left little finger, and Ruben took the opportunity to observe, "Your finger, or your life. What do you say?"

"But how does it work? Will it hurt? Will I be asleep?"

With the fingers of his right hand, Ruben began to pick at the hat that he had set down next to the tray. He seemed to be concentrating on an invisible speck of lint on its brim, and, in the meantime, he replied, "No, you'll be awake. At the Club, they pay to bite and tear off strips from living bodies, from conscious persons who are perfectly aware of what's going on. "It's part of their pleasure. I can't tell you how much it costs to be able to bite, tear off, and chew a man's finger, but I know Lambertini will hand seven thousand euros over to you when you're done." He rubbed his nose nonchalantly. "As far as hurting goes . . . well, yes, it hurts. That's only logical. But when your own life's at stake, that's something that can be endured. A male or female nurse, who follows every stage of the process, is always present and takes care that the 'eaten' does not lose consciousness. And the wounds are kept clean to avoid infection."

"And what do they use? Scalpels? Pliers?"

"Their teeth, basically. Sometimes they make use of some appropriate surgical instruments, mainly for the bones. But the fact is that it's actually the act of eating, the ability to use mouth and teeth that make it all so very, very . . . attractive. For those who find such things attractive, that is."

Mauro dropped his elbows heavily against the table, joined his hands as if in prayer, and lay his chin gently over them. He was staring at his companion, but rather as if he were viewing a world of horror opening up far beyond him. "Really . . . there are people who pay to eat human flesh?"

Ruben sighed as he raised his eyebrows. "I'm afraid so. There are those who eat in the real sense of the word, that is, to speak frankly, they swallow by the mouthful; whereas others are content with stripping off bits of meat in little bites, and then spitting them out into a receptacle. It takes all kinds."

Mauro pushed his glass, still half-full, away. His expression became hard, yet thoughtful. "And if, in theory, I accept . . . I mean, if at the moment I then change my mind . . ."

Ruben planted a look on him that would have extinguished a candle's flame.

"Enough playing around, Mauro. If you accept and I bring you to the Club, there will be no turning back. You would not be allowed. Whoever sets foot in there does so to eat or be eaten, at least for once. And for now, I don't think you need to know anything else." He grabbed his hat and put it on, tilting the brim as before. He then removed a business card from his pocket and handed it to Mauro. "Here's my number. Think it over, and if you choose this path, call me tomorrow afternoon. In the evening, I'll bring you to the Club, you'll do what you have to do, and I'll take you back. If, on the other hand, you want to ignore this offer, then good luck. Do you need a ride home?"

"No, no, I'll walk, thanks." Mauro threw a dark look at the card the other had left with him, and then it disappeared into his shirt pocket.

"Great, then. Come on, and we'll let our good friend finish his work." Ruben got up and slipped a twenty beneath a glass. "We're done," he said in a loud voice directed at the shadows massed behind the bar. "I thank you also on behalf of the Duke."

The folding door creaked open, but by the time the bartender, swaying and mumbling, had lumbered back into the bar, Ruben had already gone, and Mauro had disappeared right behind him.

The old apartment building was like a concrete beehive, fallen asleep. Mauro climbed the stairs with the slow steps of a man condemned to death (the elevator had broken down almost a month before). When he reached the landing of the fourth floor, he drew near to the door of his apartment, and, for a few seconds, placed his head against it, keeping his eyes closed.

For the entire way home, he seemed to be floating, his feet stepping over a fog bank, a hazy carpet of smoke and ashes, all that remained of the thoughts that had been burning within his brain. It was . . . it was inconceivable. All of it. The things this Ruben had told him about were beyond his comprehension. Not that he had ever had a particularly vivid imagination nor a deep knowledge of the world and all of its possible insanities, but . . . *Club Magritte? Bloody hell!* Moreover, on the other side of the scale, a very precise question remained: *Do you have, perhaps, a choice?* Maybe he even had one, *you never know*. But with an ultimatum of forty-eight hours breathing down his neck, it was difficult, really difficult.

He pulled his keys from his pants pocket, and although Mauro wasn't the least bit drunk, he fumbled around, aiming randomly at the lock as if he were. Suddenly, he was assaulted by a wave of hatred against all the people sleeping and dreaming all around him, people who cared absolutely nothing about the absurd mess into which he had fallen. Could he blame them? No, certainly not. Neither did he care anything about them, for that matter. Yet at that moment, he seemed to sense, in all of its cruelty, the indifference of the world, the weight of his own solitude. But where did they come from, these particularly foolish thoughts? Perhaps, he wondered, fear brings a heightened sensibility.

Once inside, he closed the door softly behind him, turned on the dim light in the entryway, and slipped out of his coat. The smells from the evening meal were still stagnating in the darkness, a pungent odor of garlic and wine that severely tested the tolerance of his stomach. He would have been happy if he could drop into bed just as he was, without having to go into the bathroom, without having to undress, without making the slightest noise. But even the mere act of thinking seemed to him to create the sounds of creaking and scraping. His mother would wake up, of that he was sure.

He had to pass by the bedroom of a woman who, habitually, never closed the door all the way, but left it ajar by a few inches. Mauro continued forward on tiptoe, as he was accustomed to doing in these instances, but when his mother's hoarse voice drifted from the shadows through the open crack, he was not surprised.

"Mauro?"

He halted, his head down. From the moment he had entered the house, a fierce migraine had begun to grind away inside his head. "Yeah?"

"Mauro, are you okay?"

I'm just fantastic, Mom. In two days, I'm likely to be a corpse.

"Yeah, I'm fine. Sorry if I woke you up."

"No, you didn't wake me up. I haven't managed to get to sleep yet. Do you know what time it is?"

Mauro lifted his head, directing his eyes to the hallway ceiling, an opaque nullity that hung over everything. "Midnight? Come on, Mom, get to sleep."

"It's almost three," and then silence. A silence heavy with disapproval and reproach. In his head, during those few moments, Mauro heard all of that. Those few inches of darkness spewed a caustic judgement of his life all over him, and, as always, he let it go. His mother managed to inject her poison even when she kept silent, and it was a sad and terrible thing that a part of him could understand and agree with her.

"Goodnight," and the tone of his voice was flat, without emotion. As he headed toward his own room, he heard only the disdainful rustling of a body abruptly changing position beneath the sheets.

He fell onto the bed dressed as he was, shoes included, inadvertently assuming the position of a laid-out corpse, and he fixed his eyes on the dark ceiling, persistently driving away every thought. He seemed to have been thinking far too much, and he felt as if his brain were overflowing with thumbtacks pressed against his skull. He wanted only to fade away, nothing else.

He managed to fall asleep around dawn, without realizing that he had slipped into oblivion while caressing the little finger on his left hand.

Sitting on a stone bench in the municipal park, Mauro found it relaxing to watch the wavering play of light animating the surface of the small artificial pond. Those curving contours, dappled by the dark green of the foliage, so sparkling and constantly changing, instilled in him a sense of tranquility and safety. The arrangement of abstract designs varied with each blink of the eye, and he was fascinated by the idea that certain patterns would return, after untold cycles, as an identical form of itself. It was a concept that suggested an immense and unfathomable plan regulating everything, even his own life, and it would have been comforting to have been convinced of that. In truth, where he found himself just then, he could hardly detect even the semblance of order in his own being. He had gone so far, made so many mistakes, and done so many stupid things. But now . . . now . . .

That morning he had, as usual, gotten up late, and he had done his best to avoid coming across his mother and her intolerable talk. He would not deal with it. And then he left, feigning an obviously false urgency, scattering behind him fragments of sentences about an appointment, a meeting for a job. Important? Who knows? See you later, Mom . . . He realized that would be hard for her to swallow, but he made sure she would never exchange a direct look with him, and that way, he could avoid the unwelcome possibility of an interrogation.

He had taken his lunch—toast and mineral water—in a bar, and then he had wandered around until ending up in the park. There, particularly at that early afternoon hour, a sublime calm prevailed. Very few people and almost no noise, except for the steady voice of the city in the background.

Maybe it was the thought that the evening of the following day could also have been his last, but everything—every breath, every blade of grass leaning in the breeze, every bit of chirping among the branches—seemed to be cloaked in an immeasurable beauty. Bizarre impressions for a guy like him; and yet, he found himself so full of those things, he felt to be on the verge of exploding.

He took out his cellphone and Ruben's business card.

"Two things only. At the Club, we never talk about either the 'eaters' or the 'eaten,' but only about buyers and sellers, okay?"

"Okay," replied Mauro as he sat down next to Ruben. He was immediately nauseated by the aroma of the mango deodorant that permeated the interior of the blue Volvo S80, but he did not comment about it. "And the second?"

"The second is that Lambertini likes to be called 'Count.' Count Lambertini. Got it?"

Mauro nodded as he continued to stare in front of him at the road that was taking them out of the city. A wisecrack came casually out of his mouth like spit from a chaw of tobacco. "Around here, with all the counts and dukes, blue blood must be in the drinking water," and that was said if only to lighten just a little the load that was pinning him to the seat.

Ruben was not annoyed by the remark. "Yeah, but there is a slight difference. My cousin, the Duke, comes from a poor family of tradesmen, while our Lambertini is actually a real nobleman. His lineage is rather ancient, as far as I know."

Mauro shut his mouth again, unable to come up with any comment worthy of the effort of a reply. The sun had just set, and the streets were turning into dim tunnels punctuated by the tired eyes of the street lamps, the distance between them gradually growing, just as the distances opened up between the houses, the buildings, the signs of life. The evening had begun to swallow them up into its womb, and Mauro had only to keep still and wait.

They had arranged to meet precisely at eight o'clock, in the same place where Mauro should have been the night before (and the following night) to pay off his debt. The large Volvo had pulled over, and from the window, Ruben had simply asked him, "Everything all right?"

No, there's absolutely nothing here that's all right. "Yeah, we can go."

Their conversation died down almost at once, and after the exchange of remarks regarding the noble title of the man waiting for them, it became clear that neither of the two cared much about small talk. Mauro, in truth, would have had quite a few questions to ask, but when Ruben twice answered him with, "You can ask Lambertini that," he understood it would be best to hold his breath. His stomach, it seemed to him, had been replaced by a thorn bush, and he did not want to think about what awaited him. But neither could he keep from doing just that.

Ruben extended a finger into a shadowy dimness punctuated by colored LEDs, turning on the radio. The silvery murmur of a classical symphony spread at once throughout the interior. Mauro could not tell what piece the passage was from, but he wasn't going to ask him about it nor, after all, did it matter to him. He turned his eyes to the window on his right and fixed them on the glass.

His mind returned to the car's interior only when they began an ascent accompanied by a sudden shift into a lower gear. Until that moment, the fitful streaks of sporadic lights and the dark, stringy shapes into which the world had been reduced had lulled his mind into a sort of torpor. So many mental pictures were intruding between those increasingly unrecognizable afterimages and the reflection of his astonished face. He thought he recognized the eyes of Sylvia, his ex-wife, camouflaged behind a pair of distant headlights, and Beatrice's slender, sensual hands hidden among a tree's branches, and then from its leaves dozens of birds, darker than the night, lifted off into flight, forming spindly flocks that were perhaps the fingers from those same hands, detached.

Mauro was startled when he looked at the digital clock on the dashboard. Almost an hour had passed since they had left, and now that they had reached the hills, the Volvo was probing with its headlights the asphalt ribbon that was rising and penetrating into the middle of the woods. There was no more music, only the muffled rumble of the engine, droning monotonously in his ears.

"Are we almost there?" he asked, his words a bit slurred.

Ruben looked at him as if he had forgotten he was there. "Oh, yeah, we're very close now. Five minutes and we'll be at Villa Lambertini."

Villa Lambertini, the Count, Club Magritte. Mauro felt his heart growing heavy. What was he doing? What had he gotten himself into? Too late to change his mind, for sure. Could he cast a spell, disappear on the spot? That alone would save him.

"To hell with it," he muttered.

"I'm sorry?"

Rubbing his eyes, Mauro inhaled loudly through his nose. "Nothing, nothing."

As Ruben had promised, after a handful of minutes, a wide beam of milky light, appeared from around a curve, penetrating into the darkness, and the car coasted into the broad cone of illumination projected by a floodlight mounted on a turret. It stopped a few yards from a massive wrought iron gate. Closed, of course.

A stout man in uniform, some sort of security guard, emerged at once from a dark hut built into a side wall, and walking slowly, he approached the driver. The scowl on his face was that of a prizefighter getting ready to annihilate an opponent. His right hand was poised, with feigned indifference, on the holster hanging from his belt.

Ruben lowered the window, and a gust of fresh air immediately greeted his words. "We're here for copies of the *Golconda* painting."

The guard, with his rounded and pockmarked face, seemed to be weighing the information for an instant before answering, "And how many of them do you want?"

"All of those that are in the trunk."

The man nodded, and his features relaxed dramatically. "Who should I announce?"

"Ruben De Castro with Mauro Ridolfi."

A small radio transmitter appeared from the guard's uniform pocket. He took several steps backward, sounded out their names in a low voice, then turned to disappear into his station. A few seconds later, the huge gate began to grind open. Ruben closed the window, with two fingers gave the semblance of a military salute in the direction of the darkness, and calmly drove the Volvo along the gravel drive that, after a double curve, led them to the front of Villa Lambertini.

In other circumstances, Mauro would have stayed behind to admire the luxurious cars, shining and arrogant, parked in the square opposite the building, just as he would have filled his eyes gazing at the opulent façade of the two-story building and at the curving dual staircase that led from the courtyard to the main entrance and at the almost dazzling play of lights from the balconies and the roof created by the headlight's beams. A grand celebration could have been said to be underway even if the shapes moving behind the spacious curtains cloaking the vast front windows had not been visible. But music and voices coming from some indefinite space could be heard, sounds that were suddenly amplified once Mauro opened the door and stepped out to offer his sweaty skin to the crisp night air.

Ruben handed the keys of the Volvo, along with a folded banknote, over to a young man in a gray uniform and a chauffeur's cap from earlier times. Bowing his head, the man thanked him and quickly climbed behind the wheel to take care of the parking.

"Come on. We're going this way."

Mauro, shaking himself from his drowsiness, saw that Ruben was beckoning him to follow toward a side door down from the main entryway, around the left corner of the villa, and he had the distinct impression that he was traveling inside a gigantic glass bubble full of a transparent but dense liquid. As he was walking, stepping over gravel bathed in cold halos of light, laughter and silvery notes crept into his head, but his brain did not just then have the resilience to process that data and turn it into a recognizable pattern. The effort to push aside thoughts about the reasons that had led him to that place was becoming almost unbearable.

Ruben approached a thin, dark man who had appeared next to the side entrance, and Mauro listened to them conferring. He supposed that another exchange of passwords was underway, since within a few seconds the anonymous man opened the door and stepped aside, allowing them to enter.

"Come on, follow me. The Count's waiting for us," Ruben told him in a tone of some urgency, and noticing the fog in Mauro's eyes, he snapped his fingers in front of his face. "Are you there?"

"I'm here, I'm here," replied Mauro, a bit annoyed, and then he quickened his pace, slipping into the shadow to lose himself inside the villa.

Ruben was hurrying confidently through corridors and upstairs, and along the way, Mauro tried not to remove his eyes from the nape of his neck. Muffled sounds of laughter and music, flowing from indeterminate wings of the villa, were still apparent, but the noise of their footsteps along the marble floors and the echoes that this pounding raised, had the power to overwhelm the festive sounds in the distance. Mauro did his best to keep pace. Vague images of furnishings and ornamental plants streamed by the edges of his vision, together with paint‑ings whose titles were unknown to him but which he had seen before (boulders suspended in the sky, men with umbrellas and bowler hats, sailing ships, shrouded heads), all illuminated by antiquated appliqués that flooded every space with a glare the color of brass.

When Ruben stopped, Mauro barely missed running into him.

They had reached a small room, completely empty with the single exception of a little couch positioned beneath a closed window. It had the look almost of a waiting room, with double doors shut at its far end.

"Are you ready?" Ruben asked him in a whisper.

Mauro assented with a slight move of his head. An invisible fist was holding his stomach tightly in its grip, and he felt that his left little finger had suddenly become numb.

"Good," and Ruben approached the doors and knocked. Three brisk taps then, right after, a fourth.

Mauro took a breath deep enough to make him dizzy, and when, from the other side of the door, a decisive "Come in!" was heard, he considered the possibility of turning around and fleeing, even if he doubted he would have known how to find his way out. And when Ruben opened the door, he could do no more than follow him.

The room where they were received must have been spacious, even if, in fact, it wasn't easy to determine its true scale. Two elegant table lamps placed at the ends of an imposing desk of inlaid wood provided sufficient light, warm and relaxing, but certainly not enough to reach even the side walls.

Seated behind the desk was a man in his seventies. He was bald, and with his well-trimmed mustache and goatee, he immediately reminded Mauro of an old photo of the writer, Gabriele D'Annunzio. The light from the lamps, reflected in his eyes, transformed them into a pair of bright, liquid points illuminated by the presence of an uncommon intelligence.

The remaining details of that space—an immense bookcase against the back wall, elongated leaves protruding from vases hidden in the dimness, paintings on the walls, heavy drapes drawn tight to conceal windows and doors—registered only fleetingly with Mauro as he stepped forward alongside his companion.

"Good to see you again, Count," said Ruben with confidence in his voice as he leaned forward to shake the hand of their host and he, still seated, took it and bowed his head slightly as a sign of recognition. "I brought Mr. Ridolfi here regarding that matter you know about."

Lambertini then glanced sharply at Mauro, who was ready to introduce himself and to offer his hand in turn. "Sir, uh . . . Count."

Lambertini's fingers were bony and apparently fragile, but the force with which he returned the greeting gave Mauro a bit of a shock. The Count stared at him with a severe expression for a few moments, as if to study him, but his features softened very quickly, and with a gracious smile, he indicated the two chairs arranged in front of the completely bare desk. Ruben sat down first, and Mauro followed him.

"So, Mr. Ridolfi," began Lambertini, "you're here for the left little finger, at seven thousand, am I correct?" His voice was soft, almost a whisper. But those simple words instantly pierced Mauro's heart.

"Yes."

With a smooth but rapid movement, the Count withdrew a sheet of paper from the desk drawer and set it in front of him as if he were an announcer and that were his playlist. He let his eyes skim over it, although it was clear he was doing it as a mere formality. "I see that your blood work went well. There are no problems."

This startled Mauro, and, instinctively, he turned toward Ruben, looking at him with an expression of alarm. "What's he saying?"

"A few months ago you were hospitalized with kidney stones, right?"

"Yes, but . . ." Mauro realized that his tongue was not cooperating.

"Doctor Larusso is a friend of the Duke," Ruben calmly explained, "and if the Duke asks a favor . . ."

The Count interrupted them, probably considering that no such explanations were relevant, nor should they be. "For us in the Club," he declared, gaining Mauro's complete attention, "it is essential that sellers who are ill are never introduced. Our buyers pay also for absolute security, particularly in regards to their health. If you had been a person at risk, we never would have accepted you. I'm guessing that you understand that."

Mauro opened his mouth but barely managed to nod.

"You should be honored to be here," continued Lambertini, folding his hands over the medical report. "Here the strictest rules of safety, hygiene, and, naturally, anonymity apply. The Club has to be able to offer full guarantees at every level to protect both the buyers and sellers."

"Sure, I understand. But . . . I was wondering . . ."

The Count moved his fingers slightly and smiled in silent anticipation.

"Here . . . I was wondering . . . what exactly do you do here?"

Their elderly host shifted away from the desk to recline against the high back of his chair. Then he planted his elbows on the armrests, keeping his fingers intertwined in front of him.

"Here," he replied emphatically, "we offer freedom. Freedom from the rigid chain links of morality, of accepted thought, of convention. Those who come to us do so to indulge their natural impulses, to satisfy needs as ancient as mankind and never completely suppressed. Hidden, perhaps, but always quite alive in each and every one of us. In varying degrees, of course. I'm supposing you've never eaten human flesh."

Mauro might just as well have laughed at that question. Instead, he only shook his head, staring at Lambertini as a mouse would before a cobra.

"But it's not only a matter of eating, no. Obviously some do it, but there are also many buyers who don't even swallow. What counts for them is the biting, the tearing with their teeth, *letting the animal loose*. And that's the point. Do you understand?"

Mauro caught out of the corner of his eye some motion from Ruben. He was idly smoothing the crease of his trousers along one thigh. This must not have been the first time he was hearing these remarks.

An intuitive thought came to him, and he followed it in a clumsy attempt to delay the fatal moment. "And all this has something to do . . . with sex?"

Lambertini laughed, nodding. "*Ecco* Freud, although no sensible person believes that psychoanalysis could clarify the mystery of the world. Those aren't my words. I'm only citing Magritte. Getting back to your question . . . well, maybe yes for some, and maybe no for others. What I mean is that certain aspects of anthropophagy or, in general, the impulse to return to the oral phase have, at its source, elements linked to the libido, but not that alone. Here we dig deep into human nature, Mr. Ridolfi. Here we recover our lost *persona*, we go on the hunt for our primeval form, we return to being truly ourselves." The tiny fires in his eyes gleamed brighter, sparked by his own words. "And what society regards as 'perversions' or 'taboo' are, in reality, no more than manifestations of the incalculable facets of our being. Club Magritte, however, was not born to provide space for all sexual inclinations considered deviant, but to certain variables, termed thus, as 'something . . . *phagy*.'"

Mauro raised an eyebrow as he began to realize how hot it was in that room.

"You see, Mr. Ridolfi, there are such things as pedophilia, necrophilia, gerontophilia . . . So, for the suffix 'philia,' substitute 'phagy,' and you will have understood what kinds of persons join our club."

Mauro tried to swallow, but in vain. He seemed to be sitting in an armchair lined with burning embers. "Geronto . . . phagy?"

"Certainly. Are you surprised? Once a young man shelled out a sum that could have bought him a sports car, and for what? To eat the breasts of a seventy-year-old woman."

"Alive?"

"Alive and screaming, my dear friend. At least until the young man had finished. It lasted almost half an hour. Necrophagy, on the other hand, pays a lot less, and there are practically no requests. The possibility of obtaining a cadaver on your own makes it unnecessary to resort to our club. And yet, for pedophagy, rather substantial checks need to be written. Anyway, as you'll have gathered, we have the means to satisfy almost any request."

Ruben coughed, perhaps tired of listening to such talk. Mauro's mind, however, was sinking into a muddy pool, slipping along an ever darker, ever more narrow channel.

He spoke in a choked voice, "But it's illegal . . . all this. Isn't it?"

The Count quit the backrest and again leaned over the desk. "I'm afraid you're right. It is, without a shadow of a doubt, at least in this place and in this time. But that does not present an insurmountable problem. If you knew the names of some of our buyers, you'd understand that we have our backs rather well covered. But enough of this small talk." Those last few words fused into a nail that pierced Mauro's heart.

"If you wish, then afterward I can show you something more and satisfy whatever curiosity you still might have. Among other things, we have two banquets scheduled tonight, and I'm sure you'll find them interesting. But for now, you are here in the capacity of a seller, Mr. Ridolfi. You need some money, they tell me, and we'll give it to you in exchange for the merchandise you're offering. The buyer for your little finger is already there in The White Room. Let's not keep her waiting any longer."

Saying that, he arose, mechanically tightening the soft belt that held closed the violet dressing gown emblazoned with the gilded monogram "AL." Ruben, too, sprung to his feet and placed a friendly hand on the shoulder of Mauro, who gave the impression of being slow in his reactions and not too steady on his feet.

"Hang in there," he whispered in his ear. "It'll go quick, trust me," and he waved the hand missing two fingers in front of his face.

Troubled, Mauro looked away, shifting his eyes casually to a painting that was hanging behind the Count, and almost without realizing it, he paused to observe it. It depicted a nude woman, apparently dead, stretched out on a divan. Several men were spying on her from a window, while others seemed absorbed in their inscrutable, shady actions.

"*The Menaced Assassin*," explained Lambertini when he noticed that moment of hesitation. "Magritte, naturally."

Mauro heard himself speaking as if his voice were coming from a tape recorder submerged under water. "Naturally, but what's Magritte got to do with all this?"

The Count kept his calm demeanor. "Nothing. It's my second passion, after what we are about to do now. Come on, this way."

They gained entrance to The White Room from the Count's office through a small door hidden behind a curtain. It was practically a clinic. There, the light spreading from a long neon tube was stark, and it bathed the space in a sheen of white gleaming off of the sterile tiled walls. Along with a pair of glass-fronted cabinets full of medicine, surgical trays and syringes, a sink, and a metal trash bin, what attracted Mauro's attention more than any other item was a singular steel chair positioned exactly in the middle of the room. It could have been mistaken for a rudimentary dentist's chair if it were not for the leather straps on the armrests, at ankle-height, and on the headrest, details that brought to mind, uncomfortably, the image of an electric chair.

Three persons were there. To the left, both in nursing gowns and waiting motionless next to a trolley heavy with medical instruments were a young man, tall and robust, with a blond crewcut, and a woman in her forties, her pitch-black hair gathered into a ponytail. To the right, settled in a chair next to a small table, was a middle-aged woman wedged into a blue pantsuit, plus-size, her makeup thickly applied, her brown hair combed back, and a gaudy pearl necklace spun in a double loop over her generous bosom. She directed a gracious smile toward the Count, but then quickly laid eyes on Mauro, who felt as if he were being subjected to a thorough MRI scan.

"Here we are," said Lambertini, with a flippant clap of his hands. "And, my dear lady, this is your seller."

Still sitting, the woman held out her hand. Mauro, after a poke in the ribs by Ruben's elbow, approached her to return the greeting. An intense floral perfume rose from her skin. "It's a pleasure. I'm Mau . . ."

"No names, for God's sake!" said the Count, interrupting him at once. "Here no one has names, least of all family names. Am I right, my lady?"

"You're absolutely right, Count," replied the woman in a velvety tone as she pressed Mauro's hand and continued to stare at him with eyes into which a certain lewdness could also have been read, if it were not for the predatory flashes that turned them instead into something disturbing and vaguely deranged.

With a nod, Lambertini signaled to the nurses. Moving forward promptly, the man gently grabbed Mauro by one arm, escorting him to the pseudo dentist's chair.

Mauro moved as if in a dream, his heart heavy, his limbs numb. A moment before sitting down, he threw a glance toward Ruben who, standing by the door, responded with a small grin and a complicit wink of an eye.

The nurse efficiently fastened the first strap to his right wrist. Then he kneeled down to bind his ankles.

"Is all this really necessary?" asked Mauro, his voice faint.

"It is," replied the Count. "Certain involuntary contractions sometimes create problems."

The nurse then went behind Mauro and, applying a light pressure to his temples, prompted him to recline and lay against the cushioned headrest as he immobilized him by tightening another strap around his forehead. In the meantime, the other nurse had lifted his left hand and washed it by scrubbing it carefully with a cloth soaked in fresh water, likely mixed with a disinfectant. As she performed that routine operation, the woman's expression remained consistently neutral, without the shadow of an emotion. Under other circumstances, it would also have been provocative.

Meanwhile, stuck in that position, Mauro had the chance to follow the Count's movements with his eyes. From a coatrack on the wall, Lambertini had taken a surgeon's gown and put it on, and once the nurse had finished with her task, he dragged a stool noisily behind him to sit down to the left of Mauro.

"We have an arrangement in force here. When a new seller shows up, I have to be the one, in my capacity as president and founder of the Club, to . . . welcome him."

Mauro felt his stomach turning to stone. A slight tremor began to spread from the tips of his toes to rise up along his calves.

"A sort of *droit du seigneur*, if you'll excuse the bizarre comparison. Now . . ."

Lambertini glanced over to the male nurse who, coming back into Mauro's line of sight, grabbed his left arm, unrestrained by any straps, and lifted it so that Mauro's hand was raised to the height of the Count's mouth. Instinctively, Mauro tested the firmness of that grip, if only to confirm that he did not have the least possibility of breaking free of it. Truly, there was no longer any way out. Having let himself be carried along by the current, there now was nothing left for him to do but to wait for his little martyrdom to be accomplished. It could never have been worse than falling into the hands of Gandhi, free to do to him whatever passed through his mind.

"Now," continued Lambertini, "I certainly won't tell you this isn't going to hurt. Obviously, it is going to hurt. But it's a matter that will be over within a quarter of an hour, perhaps even less. I will be quick, then I will yield my place to our esteemed client. All right?"

Having said that, he seized the base of the little finger, straightened it by applying pressure with his thumb beneath the middle phalanx, and drew his withered lips near as if to kiss it.

Mauro opened his eyes wide, then immediately closed them tight as he clenched his teeth and quickened the pace of his breathing. He was suddenly struck by a spasm—rolling from the base of his neck through his ears to invade beneath his skin—when he felt at the tip of his finger the moist stickiness of a tongue. He fought to keep his eyelids down, despite the intrusion of the neon brightness, and he wound up imagining the ecstatic expression that must have been painted across the old man's wrinkled face, and perhaps it was that image that turned his stomach even before the canines and premolars—mounted in a set of dentures tried and tested for that purpose—closed like a vise over nail and fingertip. A dazzling yellow lightning bolt shot from the finger to his brain, and, erupting from Mauro's throat, a brief, hoarse scream faded into a dying groan. His legs jerked forward, but the straps held them back with ease. The fingers of his right hand contracted into a fist, while his left arm struggled in vain to escape the torture. He heard a liquid sound of sucking as an impossible sensation of icy cold and at the same time unbearable heat permeated the entire limb. A sharp, snapping sound that resembled the cracking of a nutshell followed, and the instant he opened his eyes, he saw the Count pulling his head abruptly back, his lips raised over clenched teeth as he finished tearing away the last thin flap of skin that kept the little phalanx still attached to the rest of the finger. The nose, cheeks, and chin of the old man were bathed in red, and a misshapen lump of pinkish flesh caught between his incisors was dripping blood over his white gown.

The nurse loosened his grip slightly on an arm whose muscles were, by then, beginning to relax, and his colleague assisted by dabbing with gauze and cotton the stump from which Mauro's scarlet lifeblood was brazenly gushing. This small-scale hemorrhaging, however, quickly lost its force, and the woman then took the opportunity to wipe the sweat pouring from a forehead held back by a tight strap.

Mauro unconsciously began to breathe heavily, as if he were about to give birth. He needed oxygen, but at the same time, he sensed that breathing too fast was making the entire room spin. He stared at the hasty bandaging that hid the wound from him, and when he thought about why that effort seemed so temporary, he was compelled to whimper, "Enough . . . that's enough, please . . ."

He heard a metallic creaking. Someone had pressed the pedal to raise the cover of the small trash bin and was now spitting. He then heard the sound of running water, and after a few seconds, from the vague edge where his vision faded, Lambertini reappeared, busy drying his hands and face with a small towel of white terrycloth.

"No, no, no, my friend," he declared. "Business is business. You honor your commitment all the way, and the Club will honor its end as well. This lovely lady has purchased your left pinkie, with a small discount, of course, since I took the liberty of a little taste. So, brace yourself. After all, in the end, no one is going to die here. Come over here, my lady, and make yourself comfortable. It's your turn now."

The matronly buyer of his finger—who, in the meantime, had covered her blue pantsuit with a large tailor-made gown—came forward with a predatory smile on her face, and, continuing to stare into Mauro's eyes, she took the stool left free by the Count.

The nurse returned, applying again a strong grip to his arm, and with a sudden movement, his colleague made the rudimentary dressing on his finger disappear, exposing the living flesh, throbbing like glowing embers around the opaque whiteness of the bone.

Mauro groaned, and the cannibal smile of the woman at his side widened even more as her trembling mouth welcomed with sensuous desire the stump once she began to suck the blood from it.

"Drink this, it will do you some good." Lambertini had, in the meanwhile, reappeared on his right side, and he was drawing a shot glass close to his lips. "I can't sedate you because that doesn't fall within the terms of the agreement, but a spot of brandy will pick you up a bit."

Surprised by the unexpected offer, Mauro let the liquor flow down his throat and it erupted in his stomach with a burst of heat that rapidly spread throughout his body, and when he turned to watch, with clouded vision, the woman at work on his finger, he seemed to be viewing a scene from a film, a horrible film, one of those he could still turn away from if he wanted to, but then the brain takes care of filling all the gaps, drawing from the brutal reservoir of the imagination. And so, he might just as well take a look at what was happening to him.

His tormenter was now swiveling her head, methodically, to the right and to the left, carving with her teeth an increasingly red circular groove around the second knuckle, until a painful ring of blood appeared. Mauro was assaulted by the pungent stench of sweat coming from the woman's body, no longer subdued by the hypocrisy of the perfumes that covered her. She was only an animal now, and as such was feeding her most primitive nature, entrapped, with her eyes closed, in the garden of her sick delights. She was breathing heavily, moaning, and when she decided that the groove around the bone was deep enough around the bone, she clamped her teeth shut with renewed energy, and pulling with incisors and canines, she tore away skin, muscles, and tendons. The skin covering the second phalanx slipped off like a glove from his little pin of bone, and a cry exploded from Mauro, shattering against the ceiling and falling back all around like invisible meteorites of suffering. His immobilized body contracted beneath the wave of a spasm, and the nurse's hands, acting like a massive tourniquet, tightened even more around his arm.

The woman raised her eyelids in vague surprise.

"Would you prefer his mouth to be closed, my dear?" Lambertini asked her.

She refused the offer, shaking her head slowly as she continued to chew. Her livid face was the gory muzzle of a wild animal interrupted during a meal. She took her time swallowing and then replied, "Oh no, no. This way it's so much more . . . exciting."

Mauro, deciding not to give her further satisfaction, fixed his eyes on a sky he could not see. The light from the neon lamp filled them with tears. He then closed them again and felt himself slipping backward, head over heels, weightless, plunging into a pool of red waters.

Then the woman's mouth clamped firmly around the last remaining phalanx, and Mauro felt nothing more.

An intolerable, pungent odor brought him back to consciousness like a slap in the face. A fit of retching snapped his head forward, but nothing came up from his stomach.

"Oh, here he is. Welcome back!" Lambertini's tone was jovial as he screwed a cork back into a vial. "You can't hold out against the old ammonia salts."

Mauro was aching everywhere and he moved with caution. He was still sitting in the armchair, in The White Room, but the straps had been unfastened. A hot tingling in his left hand suddenly claimed his attention, and he noticed then the bandage, intertwined beneath his four surviving fingers, neatly and carefully wrapped around his wrist and palm.

"My compliments to you," the Count told him. "You handled yourself rather well. Certainly, it would have been better if you hadn't passed out at the end, but we can't expect too much, can we?"

Mauro looked around. The woman who had eaten his finger was no longer there. The two nurses, intent on putting their things back in place, had casually turned their backs on him.

Ruben, who had taken the place previously occupied by the buyer, was showing him an upraised right thumb.

"Now," continued Lambertini, "it is my custom to respect, without delay, agreements with my clients. Therefore . . ." From one baggy pocket of his dressing gown, he removed an envelope and offered it to Mauro, who, with a trembling hand, grabbed it. "Fourteen five-hundred bills, as agreed. I'm hoping you will not do me the discourtesy of counting them."

Mauro stared at the envelope. He felt as if he were in a daze, just as if he were gradually recovering from dental anesthesia. Stunned, chilled because of his drying sweat, and uncertain, he looked down at his left hand. His little finger no longer existed. It had been sacrificed for him, he thought, stupidly. To save his life. He would learn to live without its help, always remembering it fondly. He had not yet thought about what to tell his mother, how to explain to her why there was now one less figure there. But something would come to mind. The single notion that everything was over with seemed to be a marvelous one. Even if his mouth was not responding properly to stimulus, a dumb little smile was straining the muscles of his face.

"Are we finished?" he asked. "Can I go?" Having said that, he made an effort to get up, and Ruben quickly moved over to help him.

"Bravo," he said in a low voice. "Very well done."

"My dear sir," said Lambertini, "I really believe that you now have the right to know something more, about our Club. Would you like to take a little tour? I assure you that it will be an interesting experience, and instructive."

Mauro, by now upright on his own legs, looked to Ruben, who shrugged his shoulders as if to say, "Why not?"

"All right," he said, folding the envelope and tucking it inside his shirt. He had not counted the money, out of respect but also because he was certain it would be all there. The nightmare of the Duke and of Gandhi seemed to him to have lost all substance. And then a strange idea infiltrated his thinking . . .

Lambertini led Mauro and Ruben through several corridors, their walls hung with brightly colored prints. Always only Magritte, as expected. They then entered an elevator, and there, in that cramped space, despite the widespread scent of lavender, Mauro was also able to detect a faint smell of urine. He looked down. He was wearing dark pants, and nothing at all was apparent. But he remembered having lost control for a second during the ordeal. Embarrassing yet more than understandable, and if Ruben and the Count had noticed, they gave no indication of it.

They went down, however, only one floor, ending up finally in a room that had all the appearance of a small control center.

A dozen monitors, all turned on, showed the images transmitted in real time from the closed-circuit television cameras scattered about almost everywhere, both inside and outside the villa. A computer operator in uniform was seated in front of the console, and when the three entered, he turned to greet, with respect, the lord of the house and his two guests before swiveling back to stare somberly at the flickering wall of screens.

"Right here, you can get an idea of how the operation is managed," the Count explained directly to Mauro. "This small room represents, virtually, the watchful eye of the Club. Do you see that?"

Mauro, who, up until that moment, had been moving and thinking on a narrow track and was still too confused to analyze or evaluate anything around him, made an effort to focus his attention on those glowing, greenish rectangles, those phosphorescent pictures suspended in the half-light.

The first three, toward the upper right, were sending back sequences from the outside, motionless scenes, vaguely ghostlike, alternating in cycles: the parking area, the gate, a small garden, a back entrance. Various views capturing the inside of the building followed: empty rooms; stairways; hallways, shot from above, that drifted off into odd passages for escape; parlors and halls where men and women in elegant dress were circulating and chatting. In contrast, the monitors on the lower level offered far less ordinary images.

Mauro was not aware he had opened his mouth wide as his eyes filled up with sights that could have been viewed in a military hospital after a battle. Lying on an indistinct number of cots, human bodies, half-covered by sheets, were stirring or stretched motionless or quivering as if in the throes of unnatural fevers. Branching off from almost all of them were one or more tubes connected to an IV or other machinery. Some of them were shaking their heads back and forth, leaving black rings on their pillows. Others left their arms dangling over the edges of the cots, and still others kept their eyes and mouths open, and from the muscles tensing around their throats, it was clear that they were screaming. Mauro was grateful for the fact that the audio channels were not on.

"These," commented Lambertini, "we consider to be a little like . . . our stockpile. You see, the Club offers the possibility to sell not only parts of your own body, but even other persons, in their entirety."

Mauro, frowning as he tried to remove those distressing images from his sight, stared at the Count. "Other . . . other persons?"

"Certainly, like I told you. When we acquire complete persons, we have the opportunity to sell them over again as a way of satisfying various requests. I'll explain. Someone wants to eat a hand? No problem. We are asked for an ear or a foot? Even an entire arm—and that's already been done. So, we have our stock. We take great care that they do not get infected, become ill, or die. They form our own little breeding farm. And as hard as it may be for you to believe, some of the people that you see there have offered themselves up voluntarily, to guarantee a measure of economic security to their loved ones. As for the prices, well, those also vary, of course, according to the age of the subject desired. The leg of a child, for example, could cost over . . ."

Mauro raised a hand, a horrified expression on his face. The Count, giving proof of his keen understanding, instantly cut off his sentence. "I beg your pardon if I've been too explicit. You'll understand that for us in the Club, these are simply matters of everyday administration."

Ruben, just behind Mauro, let slip a small laugh.

"Is there anything else you'd like to know about the Club? After all, considering what we've done tonight, I now consider you one of us."

Mauro thought for a moment, retrieving an idea that had dug a tiny niche in his brain, a larval thought that could not bear to keep holed up any longer in its cocoon. "But when someone intends to buy, or to sell . . . how do they contact you, find you?"

"Ah, that's very simple. One of the most direct channels is the one that brought you here, represented by one of our friends, in this case, Mr. De Castro, behind you. We have, then, a network of contacts via the Internet, very useful, and very profitable, I might add."

"You're on the Internet?"

"Nowadays, you can't do without it. Obviously, Club Magritte's pages speak only of pictorial art, offering fine-art prints for online purchase. If some unsuspecting users really want to buy artwork, we can even accommodate them, or we apologize for the unavailability of the requested product to discourage them. But if certain passwords are inserted into the order form, passwords we disclose only to those persons who have already made our acquaintance, then we can move on to some real transactions."

Mauro allowed his attention, for an instant, to be captured by the silent monitors on the left wall. In one of these, the shot changed, showing a body too tiny to belong to an adult, and the irregular cavities in the sheet suggested that perhaps not all the limbs were present. He looked away at once, and on the spur of the moment posed another question before it evaporated from his thoughts. "And if you were offered for sale . . . say, oh, I don't know . . . a woman, an elderly woman . . ."

Lambertini nodded. "It wouldn't be the first time."

"And how much would you be willing to pay?"

"Age and weight can have an effect to some extent, and also the state of health. But I can also tell you that we are, on average, at about fifty, fifty-five thousand. Why, are you interested?"

A burst of heat stung the back of his neck, pressing Mauro to stammer, "No, no, only out of curiosity, to understand . . ."

With a vivid and crafty glint in his eyes, the Count looked him over, and then he began to stare intently at the wall full of monitors. After a few seconds, he turned to face Mauro again. "Would you like to see one final thing, still? I assure you, it will be worth the effort."

Mauro made a move to consult with Ruben who, after all, was escorting him, and, then thinking he could afford a certain amount of decision-making on his own, he replied, "All right."

Lambertini glanced at his wristwatch and declared in a lively manner, "It's almost eleven, and I think the first banquet has just about begun."

"A banquet?"

"Yes, it's a formula for a special entertainment. Very interesting, you'll see. Are you coming, too?" he then asked Ruben, who showed the palms of his two hands, displaying his eight fingers as he smiled. "Sure, of course."

"So, we're agreed!" and the Count turned quickly afterward to the operator sitting in front of the screens. "We're going to

The Dark Chamber. Call Teddy and tell him to join us there in a few minutes, okay?"

"Will do, sir."

"Great . . . So, this way, please."

An instant before leaving, Mauro caught on a screen the image of a woman, lying prone on her bed, intent on chewing into the pillow, and covered by a sheet only from the waist down. The absence of her arms was painfully evident.

The three left the room and entered yet another corridor, more narrow and far more poorly lit than those they had passed through up to that moment. Mauro moved forward between Lambertini and Ruben, his head down, unable to find a harbor for thoughts that were less and less coherent and adrift. A fierce headache was surfacing, sneaking up on him, and an exhaustion without end was unexpectedly slipping between muscle and bone. He would see what the Count wanted to show him, and then he would get out of there. The image of his mother, awake in her bed, caught him by surprise. She would have waited for him, would have asked him the usual questions, and he would have given her the usual answers. He tried to imagine how she would react, the poor woman, if he had told her: *I've gotten to meet some new friends, very nice, who ate my finger. One of these days, I'll introduce them to you!*

His left hand, hot and tingling, was sending faint signals of discomfort along his nervous system. With his right, for consolation, Mauro touched the envelope that was bouncing about beneath his shirt. He realized he was very sleepy, and he thought that once home, he would not pry himself off of his mattress for at least twenty-four hours. If it weren't for his date with Gandhi, of course. That one, he really ought not to break.

The Dark Chamber, as the Count had called it, was a small space, about nine by six feet, completely bare. The only light admitted into it was what came from the hallway when they opened the door, and Mauro chanced to see that the single element distinguishing the room was a panel positioned on the wall opposite the entryway, a wooden rectangle that stood out against the grayness of the stark cement.

"Here we are, my dear Mr. Ridolfi. Come closer, this way." Lambertini extended a hand into the dimness and grabbed a metal knob attached to the panel. "You can close the door now, Mr. De Castro, please." The light coming from the hallway narrowed into a dwindling beam and vanished.

Lambertini's voice gushed from out of the now deeper darkness. "And so, let's take a look."

In the few moments of silence that followed those words, Mauro had the feeling he was hearing screams, a woman's screams, muffled and far away, that seemed to pour forth from the invisible walls around him. His heart skipped a beat. Then he heard a creaking, and at once the darkness was driven back by an orange glare that broadened little by little as the Count slid the panel to the right to reveal a wide rectangle swelling with the ancient and tribal light of open flames. And the screams of the woman seemed to increase in volume.

"Come closer, Mr. Ridolfi. This little chamber is similar to a tiny screening room. Here you look, and you fill your eyes and soul . . . to experience pleasures contemporary mankind has completely forgotten."

Mauro was really not at all certain he wanted to do it. Nevertheless, he took a step forward, bringing himself right up to the pane of glass. And he looked.

About six feet further beneath The Dark Chamber's floor level, a vast hall expanded outward to disappear in a profusion of shadowy crevices, a sort of immense subterranean crypt, supported by arches and columns of exposed stone. Various torches were burning in metallic stanchions braced to the wall, flooding with agitated shards of hellish light the spectacle that was taking place at the center of the room. Mauro took in the details sequentially, allowing his brain to put together one by one the pieces that would make up the entire picture.

At first, he saw a number of people, men and women. Six or seven, at a glance. They were wearing long, black robes and masks of the same color that partially concealed their faces from the noses up. They were gathered around a table, a wooden structure that, with its irregular shape, resembled a star. And stretched out on that table, restrained, was a young woman, nude. A young woman who was screaming. Her head and extended limbs were positioned to correspond with the five points of the star, and the persons circling around her were moving slowly, bending over, shifting a bit, stopping to observe, bending over again . . . Every movement of each of them disrupted the pattern of shadow and light on the body of the girl, revealing and hiding new details, and it took Mauro about twenty seconds to understand the full scope, the real significance of what he was seeing: they were eating her, all of them together. One bite at a time, one mouthful at a time, calmly making a shambles of her body. While that poor girl arched her spine and threw her head backward—her face glistening with sweat and her long, blonde hair spread out over the edge of the table—those deranged dinner guests attacked her with their teeth, at their leisure, tearing off small strips of flesh, chewing, spitting on the floor, wiping off their grisly faces with their sleeves. And as some were raising their heads over the ribcage or a thigh, others were lowering theirs over an arm or the pubic area, so that the torment never had the least moment of respite. The blood covering the victim in patches was trickling into a thousand streamlets to feed the dark, liquid carpet that was widening, slowly, at the foot of the table.

Mauro noticed just then the presence of a man, short and in his sixties, who was not actively participating in the banquet, but who clearly had other roles. He was wearing a white surgical gown and, equipped with a washcloth and a sponge, he was methodically cleaning off the blood from the girl's body, drying the numerous wounds (in a few places, at the top of a shoulder and beneath a devastated breast, the bones were already just visible), and there was also a moment when he quenched her thirst, allowing water—wrung out from a rag tossed afterward into a nearby bucket—to drip down through her open lips. From time to time, he also spoke in a low voice with the participants of this horrid banquet as if he were quietly giving directions or advice.

"That one is what we call a survival coach," Lambertini explained to him in a confidential tone as he tapped the end of his index finger against the glass. "His job is to ensure that the meal, that is, the girl, lasts as long as possible under such extreme conditions. Naturally, we've administered a doping agent to her so that her system will hold up longer than expected. We also have injected her with an extra pint of blood, as a precaution. In addition, the coach aids inexperienced buyers in controlling their urges, to avoid until the very end the vital parts. In short, not to do too much damage too quickly. Otherwise, much of the enjoyment is ruined. It can go on for an hour and a half if all works out well."

Mauro listened to that explanation without averting his stunned eyes from the nightmarish sight that would be spoiling for him many, many nights of sleep to come, of that he was sure. He should not have followed the Count there. He should not have seen what he was seeing.

Two sharp knocks resounded from the door in the brief pause between one scream and the next.

"Come in!" exclaimed the Count. A shaft of light from the hallway spread out behind them. Mauro instinctively looked around and saw on the threshold the silhouette of a brutish figure whose shoulders almost spanned the doorframe.

"You need me, Count?"

"Could be," replied Lambertini. "In a little while. Stay right there, Teddy. Thanks."

The man nodded and remained in the doorway, unmoving.

Mauro felt that it was really now time to get out of there. He pressed two fingers against his closed eyes, trying in vain to empty them of the horrors that had accumulated there. He was becoming nauseous, and his head had been transformed into a wineskin full of shards and nails.

"Okay, I think now . . ." he began to say.

But Lambertini interrupted him. "You would like to leave us now, am I right?"

Mauro swallowed emptily as he said, "Yes, please. I don't feel very well. I'd like to get back home."

The Count did not fail to maintain his detached demeanor of cordial goodwill, but the flames from the torches on the other side of the glass painted a less reassuring mask on his face. Sunk into his pale, tight features, his eyes had become two pinpoints of fire.

"The banquet is a special occasion here at the Club. They are not arranged very often, but when we do, it's a real feast. And tonight, like I told you, we actually have two on the program. Quite a fine occasion, don't you think? You don't want to miss the one at one o'clock."

Mauro tried to stand up to Lambertini's gaze, but the dread from the smooth tones in which those words had been spoken and from the insinuations they seemed to hide, made his legs go limp.

"Unfortunately, my dear Ridolfi," continued the Count, "you have been sold and, accordingly, we are in the position to make you available under the agreed-upon terms."

Mauro could hardly catch his breath, while the ground began to pitch like a raft beneath his feet. "What? Sold . . . who . . .?"

The Count did not reply directly, but his devious expression opened Mauro's eyes immediately, and he turned abruptly around.

Ruben was standing with his back leaning against a wall, his arms folded, and as cool and collected as ever. "Well, after what you did, what would you expect? To get out of all this with just a pinkie? I'm really sorry, but you simply can't screw around with the Duke like you did."

Mauro grit his teeth as he listened to the blood pumping furiously against his temples. "You son of a bitch!" and he made a move toward him, his right hand outstretched like a claw.

Lambertini's voice sounded out quietly. "Teddy?"

And a dark mass shifted from the threshold, thrusting an arm out forward. In the span of a second, Mauro had his neck entrapped in a clamp of nerves and muscles, and, slavering and flailing, he could do nothing else but moan. A deluge of brightly colored lights began to pour down from the dark sky that loomed over him. The room was moving, or perhaps it was only his body being carried off like a sprig of straw. He tried to fill his lungs, but his throat had been reduced to a narrow tube through which oxygen, overheated and hissing, struggled to flow. In the air, there were voices. Someone was talking, but he could not understand what was being said, because of the increasingly high-pitched drone that was now raging through his ears. So he closed his eyes and let the weariness that had settled into his soul widen and envelope him like a damp, leaden blanket.

As he hurried through the hallway of his home, he tried to avoid raising the slightest sound, although he knew that his mother was not sleeping. She was waiting for him, awake, in the dark. She would not let him pass without an exchange of words.

Pausing at her doorway, he stepped a foot or so to peer within. A faint beam of light fell directly over the woman's face and over her wide-open eyes. The two stared at each other in silence for a few moments, and then, against all expectation, the old woman lowered her eyelids and resumed the regular, hissing sound of a sleeper's breathing.

Mauro stood staring at her for yet another instant, and then he withdrew slowly, heading toward his own room.

Then, all at once, his mother's hoarse voice caught up with him from behind, having crept out from the darkness concentrated between the jamb and the half-closed door. "You know, I had this horrible dream."

Mauro stopped, shaken by a tremor. He would not have listened, but he had no way to avoid it.

"I dreamed of a painter. A painter who wanted to eat me. I recognized him. It was Magritte. And I knew it was you who had asked him to do it. What a bizarre dream, don't you think?"

Mauro's teeth began to chatter. He stood there petrified, hoping that his mother had finished. After a pause, however, the woman's voice, this time deeper, returned to assault him. "Did you want to have me eaten alive? Are you thinking about that? Are you? Are you thinking about that?"

Mauro could not take much more, and he slipped into his room, moving lightly as if others were carrying him. Then he closed the door behind him and threw himself backward onto the bed without turning on a light.

He could not prevent his teeth from chattering, as if his body temperature had collapsed. Shutting his eyes tightly, he resolved not to open them, no matter what. As long as he remained in the dark and in silence, he was safe. Nothing could have violated his internal precincts.

He had not prayed for so many years, and the prayers he managed to draw from his memory were imprecise, incomplete. But he began to recite whatever he could recall, without opening his mouth, remembering cherished phrases from his mind and heart, and then letting them roll over his tongue, one after the other, without pause.

He had the impression that the darkness beyond his eyelids, outside his body, was now dappled with flickering, reddish halos, but he was sure that such a thing would not have made the slightest difference to him as long as he did not open his eyes or make a single sound. He had to sleep. He had to remain invisible so that what was inhabiting his imagination would do the same.

Even the silence all around him had begun to fragment under the erosive action of unintelligible whisperings. No matter. It was enough to stay motionless and, above all, to keep his eyes closed. This was repeated as he held his breath. Eyes closed, and nothing would happen to him. He felt that if he let his eyes open, that which did not exist would immediately have taken bodily form, and for him, that would mean his complete ruin.

Voices? His mother, perhaps. His mother talking to herself?

Noises. Was it her? Her getting up and walking down the hallway, in the dark, bumping into furniture, stumbling, cursing . . . But she could not do anything to him, as long as he stayed there, teeth clenched, praying, safe in his room, lying on his wooden bed. He did not feel the mattress beneath him, but that was not necessarily a problem. Don't open your eyes, he told himself. Don't open them and don't try to move. But you can't do that anyway. You're tied up tight . . .

The prayer he was mumbling faded against his palette into a whimpering very close to crying.

No, it was really no longer possible to keep on pretending. He knew perfectly well how things stood.

When the feast began, and the first teeth sank into his flesh, he dropped his lower jaw, and the pain roared out from him, a pain that exploded into a red fountain against the shadows and the flames that hung over him. Only then, unable to avoid it any longer, did he open his eyes to greet the bloody masked faces from the purgatory that awaited him.

Nicola Lombardi, an active participant in the Horror Writers Association, has published in Italy the novels *The Gypsy* Spiders, *Black Mother*, *Night Calls*, *The Red Bed, The Tank, Strigarium*, and The Engraver, as well as seven collections of stories. In addition, he has published novelizations from the films of Dario Argento (*Profondo Rosso* and *Suspiria*) and translated works by Jack Ketchum, Seabury Quinn, and many others for the Italian market. In 2021 Tartarus Press published his collection *The Gypsy Spiders and Other Tales of Italian Horror* ("Lombardi maintains a nervy, churning atmosphere, keeping readers just off-balance enough to let the big beats feel shocking and subversive. . . . Lombardi has a knack for writing endings that linger. Lovers of postwar narratives and surrealist horror won't want to miss this."--*Publishers Weekly}*. Full bibliography at www.nicolalombardi.com.

J. Weintraub has published fiction, essays, and poetry in all sorts of literary places and his plays have been produced throughout the USA and internationally. As a translator he has introduced the Italian and Swiss horror writers, Nicola Lombardi and Davide Staffiero, to the English-speaking world, and his annotated translation of Eugène Briffault's *Paris à table: 1846* was published by Oxford UP in 2018. His collection of speculative fiction, *A Visit to the Catacombs*, is scheduled for publication in 2026. More at https://jweintraub.weebly.com/

INTERSTELLAR FLIGHT PRESS